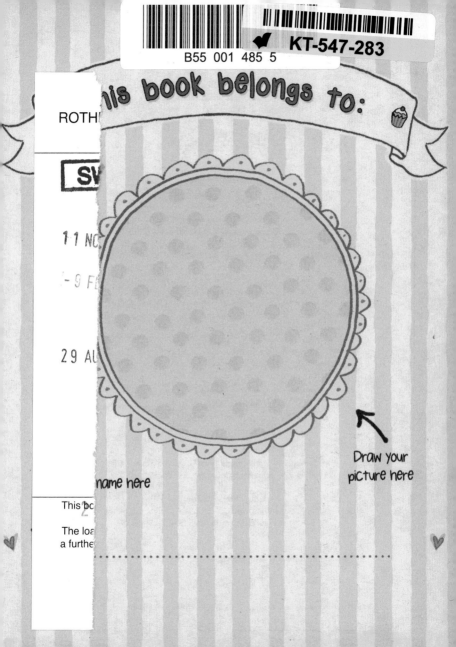

This book belongs to:

Draw your
picture here

With special thanks to Lil Chase

Ellie's Magical Bakery: A ROYAL TEA FOR ROYALTY
A RED FOX BOOK 978 1 782 95269 5

First published in Great Britain by Red Fox,
an imprint of Random House Children's Publishers UK
A Penguin Random House Company

This edition published 2015

1 3 5 7 9 10 8 6 4 2

Copyright © Ellie Simmonds, 2015
Illustrations copyright © Kimberley Scott, 2015

Penguin Random House is committed to a sustainable future for our business, our readers and our
planet. This book is made from Forest Stewardship Council® certified paper.

Set in Bembo 15pt

Red Fox Books are published by Random House Children's Publishers UK,
61–63 Uxbridge Road, London W5 5SA

www.**randomhousechildrens**.co.uk
www.**totallyrandombooks**.co.uk
www.**randomhouse**.co.uk

Addresses for companies within The Random House Group Limited
can be found at: www.randomhouse.co.uk/offices.htm

THE RANDOM HOUSE GROUP Limited Reg. No. 954009

A CIP catalogue record for this book is available from the British Library.

Printed and bound in Great Britain by CPI Group (UK) Ltd, Croydon CR0 4YY

Ellie's Magical Bakery

A Royal Tea for Royalty

ELLIE SIMMONDS

Illustrated by Kimberley Scott

RED FOX

Greyton
Woods and
Waterfall

Ellie's
Magical
Bakery

Ellie's Magical Bakery

Greyton
Green

Talia's House

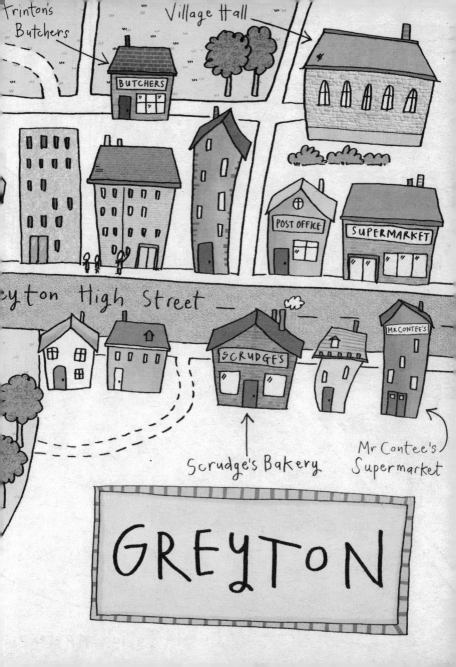

The TV Show
BRITAIN'S BESTEST BAKERS
is coming to Greyton
Auditions in the
Village Hall
First Prize — £1000
With a secret VIP judge!

Chapter 1

Ellie used a spatula to ice the last bit of the last cake she had prepared that afternoon. The icing was pink, thick and creamy. Some of it got on her finger and she licked it off.

"Delicious!" she said to herself.

"Can I have a try?" asked her best friend, Basil,

 1

racing over from the other side of the bakery. He was wearing a T-shirt with a cute puppy on the front. Basil loved animals and always wore T-shirts with pictures of animals on.

Ellie handed him the bowl and he stuck his finger in. He tasted it, then took another scoop and let Ellie's cat, Whisk, lick a bit.

"Wowweee, Ellie," Basil said. "That's your yummiest yet."

Whisk miaowed, clearly agreeing.

"Maybe we should try a whole slice?" Basil suggested, raising his eyebrows high above his glasses.

Both he and Ellie laughed. This was a trick Basil tried every day. But the cakes, biscuits and treats they baked here weren't for them to eat; they sold them to the villagers of Greyton. Greyton had once been a grey, miserable place, but it had become a lot brighter and its residents

a lot happier since Ellie's Magical Bakery opened up. So many people came into the shop to buy Ellie's brilliant bakes that she knew most of the village.

Ellie, Basil and Whisk spent their days cooking and baking. It was hard work but also lots of fun. And they had help from a tiny magical chef – Victoria Sponge. She looked like a fairy, but instead of a crown,

a pretty dress and a magic wand, she had a chef's hat, a white apron and a wooden spoon!

"Keep your hands off!" she said now, waving her

wooden spoon at them. But she was smiling too – she knew they were joking. "We have to leave the icing to set overnight. Then we'll finish the decoration off in the morning."

"What do we have to do to finish it?" asked Basil.

"I'll check the magical recipe book," Ellie replied.

The magical recipe book was a gift from Ellie's father. He'd been a baker and Ellie remembered his ginger beard, round cheeks and silly deep chuckle.

Every time she thought of him she was surrounded by the aroma of freshly baked cakes. He had died a few years ago, but had somehow arranged for Ellie to receive a recipe book on her birthday. It was no ordinary recipe book, though: the recipes inside were always just the very ones she needed. When Ellie followed the instructions, magical things happened.

She looked down at the book, which lay open on the worktop. This cake was called *A Cake for the Number One Bakery*. So far they had followed the recipe exactly – all except for the last step:

Once the pink creamy
icing has set, write

But the rest of the page was blank.

"The recipe's not finished!" Basil exclaimed, pushing his hair back so that it stuck up on end.

7

"What does it want us to write?" Ellie asked Victoria Sponge. "Why won't it tell us?"

The magical baker flew over, leaving a trail of glitter behind her. She looked down at the book, but still the final instruction wouldn't appear.

"How very odd . . ." She hovered around Ellie's head, making Ellie's long brown hair fly up. "Maybe the book thinks we've worked hard enough for one day."

"I think so too," said Ellie, grinning.

"I think so three," said Basil.

"Miaow," said Whisk, just to join in.

"What should we do now? I wonder . . ."

But there was a twinkle in Victoria Sponge's eye. She knew what Ellie would say.

"Let's go swimming!" Ellie and Basil cried out at the same time.

Victoria Sponge took her place on the front cover of the magical recipe book and winked up at Ellie. Ellie tucked the book

into her backpack, left the cake on the worktop to set, and turned off the lights in the bakery.

"Get your swimming things and we'll meet poolside in ten minutes," she said to Basil once the shop was all locked up.

"OK!" said Basil, who had already started up the high street.

Ellie had her swimming things ready in her backpack, so she made her way to the woods, looking forward to a refreshing swim.

Ellie powered through the water, kicking her legs and windmilling with her arms. She kept her head down, only turning it when she needed to breathe.

The pool was in a hidden part of the woods not far from the village. A small waterfall trickled down a rocky slope and gathered at the bottom. It was one of Ellie's absolutely favourite places.

Finally she reached the edge and turned to Basil, who was sitting on the rocks with his feet in the water. His bright red

swimming trunks had dolphins on them.

He looked at Ellie, then checked his stopwatch, then looked at Ellie again, as if he couldn't believe his eyes.

"Wowweee!" Basil put on his glasses and stared at the stopwatch once more. "That was really fast!"

Whisk miaowed in approval.

Victoria Sponge flew over to Ellie. "You really are a very good swimmer, Ellie," she said.

"Thank you," Ellie replied. "My dad taught me."

"He'd be so proud of you," said Victoria Sponge. Ellie knew that the magical little baker had been very good friends with her dad.

"I love swimming," she said, "almost as much as I love baking. When I watched the Olympics, I was amazed how speedy all the swimmers were. I've always dreamed of swimming at the Aquatics Centre

in the Olympic Park one day."

"I could take you there if you like," said Victoria Sponge.

It was a lovely offer, but Ellie sighed sadly. "Thanks," she said, "but my aunt and uncle would never let me have a nice treat like that."

Since her dad died Ellie had been forced to live with her horrible aunt, uncle and cousin Colin Scrudge. The Scrudge family had moved into Ellie's dad's bakery and changed its name to Scrudge's Bakery. They were supposed to look after Ellie and the shop, but they weren't doing a very good job of either.

She heaved herself out of the water and Basil handed her a towel patterned with multi-coloured cupcakes. "Speaking of my aunt and uncle," she said, "I'd better go home."

Basil looked at his watch again and his eyes widened. "Me too! It's almost time for tea." He quickly pulled his puppy T-shirt on over his head.

When Ellie was dry, she got out her magical recipe book. Victoria Sponge flew up and landed on the front cover so that Ellie could carry her home.

Ellie, Basil and Whisk walked back down Greyton High Street. Ellie waved at the postwoman, Mrs Pearson, as she went past. She had curly blonde hair, and whenever Ellie made chocolate éclairs at

the bakery, Mrs Pearson always bought two.

Mrs Pearson waved back. "Hello, Ellie! Hello, Basil!"

Whisk miaowed.

"And hello to you too, Whisk," she added. "Isn't it a lovely day? Not a cloud in the sky, or a hint of a breeze."

But all of a sudden a huge gust of wind

came out of nowhere, blowing Ellie's thick brown fringe away from her face. A piece of paper fluttered across the pavement and landed directly in her path. Then, as quickly as it had started, the wind stopped.

Ellie picked up the piece of paper.

The TV Show
BRITAIN'S BESTEST BAKERS
is coming to Greyton
Auditions in the
Village Hall
First Prize — £1000
With a secret VIP judge!

Basil read it over Ellie's shoulder. "Wowweee," he said. "It was as if the flyer *wanted* you to pick it up."

Mrs Pearson read it too. "They're coming tomorrow. If you get through the audition, you get an all-expenses-paid trip to take part in the grand final on TV. And it's held in the Olympic Park in London."

All at once Ellie had a brilliant idea. A grin spread over her face.

"Are you going to enter, Ellie?" Basil asked. "You'd definitely win."

She was still smiling, but she shook her head. "I have a different plan."

Basil looked confused, but Ellie didn't stop to explain. She waved goodbye to Mrs Pearson and started running down the high street, with Basil and Whisk following close behind.

When she reached Scrudge's Bakery and pushed open the door, she was hit by a horrible smell – rotting lettuce and unwashed underpants.

Revolting, as usual, she thought.

"Aunt! Uncle!" she called.

The shop was dirty and the shelves were filled with mouldy old cakes. Mrs Scrudge sat slouched behind the till. She never moved – there were never any customers to serve.

"Oh, it's you," she sneered.

"What's all this noise?" Mr Scrudge pushed open the door from the kitchen. He was a huge man, about the size of

a garden shed, and he had very bad breath. He frowned down at Ellie. "What do *you* want?"

"Something stupid, I bet," said Colin, appearing too. Colin was Ellie's cousin. He was twice as mean as his parents, and three times as greedy. "Ellie only says stupid things."

Ellie ignored Colin and smiled politely up at her uncle. "I wanted to show you this." She waved the flyer in front of him.

Basil shook his head. "Ellie," he whispered. "Don't tell them."

Mr Scrudge snatched the flyer out of her hand. His mouth made an O shape.

"One thousand pounds!" he gasped.

"And there's a trip to London," Ellie added, looking at her aunt. "All expenses paid."

Mrs Scrudge's eyes lit up.

She snatched the piece of paper from Mr Scrudge, who scowled at her.

"Ellie," Basil whispered again, "why are you showing the Scrudges?"

"And the whole thing will be on TV," Ellie added, ignoring Basil's protests. Telling the Scrudges about the competition was part of her plan.

"There's going to be a secret VIP judge!" Mrs Scrudge exclaimed, clapping her hands together.

Ellie's plan was working.

"I don't think we should bother." Colin had turned a little pale.

Ellie was surprised. Her cousin was usually so confident.

"Shut up, Colin," said Mr Scrudge.

"But . . ." Colin started.

His parents weren't listening. They were too busy planning what they were going to do in London and how they were going to spend the prize money.

Basil leaned over and whispered to Ellie. "I don't understand," he said. "Why would you want *them* to enter the competition? You should enter it for yourself!"

Ellie grinned at her friend. "But if Scrudge's Bakery wins the competition, my aunt and uncle will have to go to the Olympic Park in London. Then I can go swimming in the Aquatics Centre!"

Basil shook his head in amazement. "Wowweee," he said. "That's genius!"

Then he scratched his head thoughtfully, making his hair stand on end. "There's only one problem: the Scrudges' cakes are awful! How are they ever going to win?"

Ellie looked down at her backpack, where the magical recipe book was hidden. "We're going to have to help them," she said. "In secret."

Chapter 2

Greyton Village Hall looked beautiful. There was bunting strung across the ceiling, as well as fairy lights and posters about *Britain's Bestest Bakers*. The room

was packed with people from Greyton – some entering the competition, some who had just come to watch; all of them wore their nicest clothes and looked very smart, hoping to get on TV.

Ellie managed to find a free table in the middle and set her box down on it.

She had baked something special from her magical recipe book – *Royal Tea for Royalty*: scrumptious scones filled with

cream and jam. Ellie thought the name was funny, but she wasn't sure if her scones would win. However, Victoria Sponge had suggested that Ellie should use this recipe, and she always knew the right thing to do.

Mr Patel walked past holding a gigantic chocolate pie. It had sections of white and milk chocolate on it, and was covered with sprinkles. Ellie's mouth watered just looking at it.

"Hello, Ellie," he said brightly. "Are you entering the competition today?"

Ellie shook her head. "I'm holding this table for my aunt and uncle." She put out the sign she'd made. It read:

Scrudge's Bakery

Mr Patel looked as disappointed as Ellie felt. She wished she could enter the competition for herself.

Just then, the Scrudges arrived.

"Out of my way." Mr Scrudge barged in, pushing people aside as he walked through the hall. "Make way for the

winners!" He wasn't wearing his best clothes – he looked filthy!

Mrs Scrudge waddled along behind him. "You might as well go home now!" she said with a cackle.

The people of Greyton shrank back as the Scrudges passed by.

Colin walked slowly behind his parents, his head bowed low. Was it Ellie's imagination, or did he look embarrassed?

"Uncle! Auntie!" Ellie waved at them. "I saved you a table."

The Scrudges shuffled over to her.

"Oh, Ellie," said Mrs Scrudge, smirking.

"You're so small I almost didn't see you there."

"You're not entering with those things, are you?" asked Mr Scrudge, looking at her box of scones. "They're small and stupid – just like you!"

Ellie had a condition called Achondroplasia, which meant that she was shorter than most people. But she certainly wasn't stupid – and she knew that she was a far better baker than either of the Scrudges.

They pushed her out of the way and plonked their cake tin down on the table. Ellie moved her box of scones onto the chair behind it.

"A thank you would be nice," Basil muttered.

"Did I hear something?" said Mrs Scrudge with a nasty grin.

Mr Scrudge opened his tin to reveal the

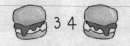

most disgusting cake Ellie had ever seen –
and having lived with the Scrudges, she'd
seen a few! It looked more like a splat than
a cake. It was dark brown, but not because
it was made of chocolate; it looked like it
had been kicked along the floor and got
covered in dirt. There were tiny little teeth

marks around the edges where rats must have nibbled it. They hadn't nibbled much of it, though. Even the rats didn't want to eat the Scrudges' cakes!

But Ellie wasn't worried; she and Basil had a plan.

She winked at Basil and he winked back. He straightened up his T-shirt and cleared his throat. Today his T-shirt had a cow on it; the cow was happily chewing away on some grass.

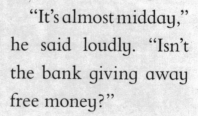

"It's almost midday," he said loudly. "Isn't the bank giving away free money?"

Mr Scrudge's head snapped up. "What?"

"Oh, that's right," Ellie said. "The new bank on the high street is giving away hundred-pound notes to everyone who comes—"

She hadn't even reached the end of her sentence before Mr Scrudge and Colin disappeared out of the hall.

It was going to plan! All Ellie had to do now was swap their cake for her cream and jam scones. Hopefully then the Scrudges would win

and Ellie would be on her way to the Olympic Park in London.

She turned to her best friend. "Good work, Basil. Now—"

But her aunt was still there, too lazy to move. If she didn't leave, there was no way Ellie could swap the cakes. She could see the judges at the other end of the hall. There was the mayor of Greyton, who judged the village's baking competition every year, and an official-looking woman in a suit, holding a notepad, with a pencil tucked behind her ear. She was the producer of the television programme.

It wouldn't be long before they reached the Scrudges' table.

"I'll go and see if I can stall them," Basil whispered, and he ran off towards the judges.

"Why don't you go and have a look at some of the other entries, Auntie?" Ellie said quickly.

"Nah," said Mrs Scrudge with a flap of her flabby hand. "Can't be bothered."

Then she pulled back the chair – the chair where Ellie had hidden the scones . . . Ellie opened her mouth to say something, but it was too late. With a large *thump* and a *squish*, Mrs Scrudge sat on Ellie's box. Cream and jam splattered out of the sides, all over the floor.

The scones were ruined. There was no way the Scrudges could win now! Ellie wouldn't be going to London after all.

Chapter 3

Ellie's plan had failed. She looked down at the Scrudges' disgusting cake.

"What am I going to do, Whisk?" Ellie whispered to her cat.

He rubbed against her legs comfortingly, then rubbed up against Ellie's backpack, making it fall over. Her magical recipe book slipped out.

"Clever cat!" Ellie said, scratching him

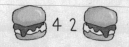

behind the ears. "I'll ask Victoria Sponge
– she'll know what to do."

Ellie crept over to a quiet corner of the
hall. Luckily everyone had their eyes on
the judges, who were now tasting Mr
Patel's entry.

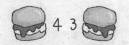

"And what is this called?" the lady with the pencil behind her ear was asking him.

"I call it *Chocolate Perfection Pie*," he told her.

The lady nodded at the mayor, a knowing smile on her face. "I know our secret VIP judge will love this," she said.

With everyone's attention elsewhere, Ellie opened her recipe book and whispered, "Victoria Sponge?"

Just saying the words seemed to work some sort of spell: the little baker began to peel out of the book. She flew up and landed on Ellie's shoulder.

"How can I help, Ellie?"

Victoria Sponge's Magical Recipe Book

Ellie explained about Mrs Scrudge sitting on her scones, and Victoria Sponge frowned. "Oh dear!" she said. "I might be able to fix the problem, but we need to get Mrs Scrudge out of the way so that I can work my magic."

"OK," said Ellie, "I'll see what I can do."

Victoria Sponge tucked herself behind Ellie's long brown hair so that no one could see her. Ellie headed back to where her aunt was sitting.

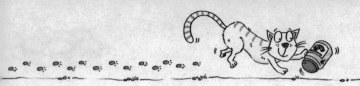

"It looks like you're sitting on something, Auntie," she said. "I think some careless person must have left their cake box on your chair."

Mrs Scrudge bent over with an *Oof!* "So they have!" she exclaimed.

"Why don't you go and clean yourself up?" suggested Ellie.

Mrs Scrudge shrugged. "Nah," she said. "These squashed cakes make a comfy cushion."

Mrs Scrudge wouldn't budge!

Basil came back to the table. He was holding something in his hand.

Mrs Scrudge frowned at him. "What have you got there?"

Basil took a bite of a large cupcake smothered in glittery icing. "Mrs Noonan is giving out free samples of her cupcakes."

Mrs Scrudge suddenly jumped up out of her seat as if she had been stung by a bee. "Free cupcakes!" She shoved Basil out of the way and ran off to find them.

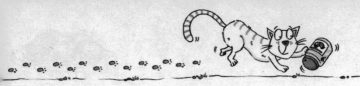

Ellie had never seen her aunt move so fast! "Well done, Basil!" she cried. "That was a brilliant plan!"

Basil swallowed the last bit of cupcake. "It wasn't a plan!" he laughed. "Mrs Noonan really *is* giving away free cupcakes! Here – I got you one."

Ellie laughed as she took the cupcake from him. She let Whisk lick the glittery icing off her fingers. He purred.

The judges were still on the other side of the hall, tasting one of Mrs Pearson's cookies, which were iced with white icing.

"OK, Victoria Sponge," Ellie said to the tiny magical chef. "The coast is clear."

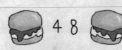

Victoria Sponge flew up, flapping her golden wings and leaving a trail of glitter behind her. She hovered over the Scrudges' cake, grimacing as she looked down at it. "Phew!" she said, holding her nose. Then she pulled the tub of magical baking dust out of her apron pocket. "This brings out the deliciousness in everything" – she sprinkled a heaped spoonful of the glittery sugar dust all over the Scrudges' cake –

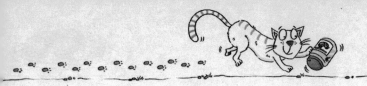

"though I'm afraid that magical baking dust alone can't fix this!"

Ellie bit her lip. "Then what are we going to do?"

"Just watch," Victoria Sponge said, a twinkle in her eye.

She twirled her wooden spoon in the air as if she was stirring an invisible mixture. The brown splat was covered in a cloud of glitter. Then it seemed to disappear.

"Victori—"

But the transformation wasn't complete yet. In its place appeared a perfect circular shape. It became pink, with thick, creamy icing.

The glitter gradually vanished and Ellie recognized the cake: it was the one they had made the day before – *A Cake for the Number One Bakery.*

She gasped. So did Basil. So did Whisk.

But then she gulped with worry. "We didn't finish it, remember?" she whispered to Victoria Sponge.

"So open the recipe book and see if the

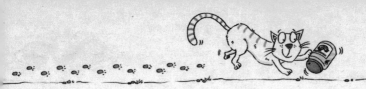

final instruction is there."

Ellie opened the magical recipe book at the right page. Where the page had been blank yesterday, she saw words writing themselves, wiggling across the page like worms.

Now it read:

Once the pink creamy icing has set, write:

SCRUDGE'S BAKERY

in white icing.

Ellie knew where she could find some white icing! She ran over to Mrs Pearson and asked if she could borrow her icing bag. The postwoman was only too happy to oblige. Victoria Sponge added a spoonful of magical baking dust to the icing, and Ellie carefully piped out the words, using her best handwriting.

And just in time too – Colin was coming back to the table, looking very cross. Quick as a flash, Victoria Sponge jumped back into the magical recipe book.

"Oi, Squirt," Colin said, glaring at Basil. "Why did you lie about the free money? Did this shrimp put you up to it?"

Ellie and Basil shrank away from him, but Colin stopped when he caught sight of the cake on the table.

"How did that . . . ?"

He stared at Ellie again. But this time he
didn't seem cross; he just looked confused.
"Did you . . . ?"

But there was no time to answer him.
The judges had arrived.

"What's this?" asked the mayor, the
gold chains around his neck rattling.
"Is this the entry from
Scrudge's Bakery?" He
looked just as surprised as
Colin – Scrudge's Bakery
was famous . . . for all the
wrong reasons! Everyone
knew that their cakes
were disgusting.

The female judge took the pencil from behind her ear and made a note in her pad. "I'm the producer from the television show *Britain's Bestest Bakers*," she said to Ellie. "A cake like this would look wonderful on TV."

The Scrudges" cake *did* look wonderful. Ellie just hoped it tasted as good.

The judges each cut a large slice and exchanged a glance before taking a big bite.

Ellie winced, waiting to see their reaction.

Basil winced.

Whisk winced.

Colin winced too, but Ellie didn't think it was just to join in. He looked really nervous.

The judges' smiles grew very wide.

"Well! What a treat!" said the mayor.

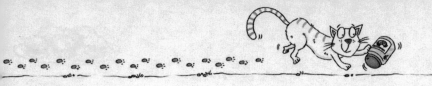

"What's a treat?" came a gruff voice from behind him.

Ellie saw the large looming shape of Mr Scrudge. He was puffing and panting, having run to the bank and back. Mrs Scrudge followed behind, sweating from waddling over from the other end of the hall.

"Is this your cake?" asked the television producer.

Mr Scrudge peered down at the perfect pink cake; he looked puzzled. "Ummm . . ."

"Because it's the nicest cake I have ever tasted!" the woman said, waving her pencil around in front of her.

"Of course it's my cake!" said Mr Scrudge.

"It's got our name on it, hasn't it?" Mrs Scrudge was as pink as the icing.

"There are no more cakes to try,"

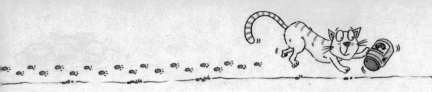

the mayor said. "I declare Mr Patel and Scrudge's Bakery the winners of today's auditions."

Mr Scrudge whooped and Mrs Scrudge squealed. However, Colin did not look pleased. Ellie couldn't think why.

She turned to Basil and grinned. "Hooray! I'm going to London!" she said with a smile. "I'll see the Olympic—"

"Who said anything about *you* going to London?" interrupted Mrs Scrudge.

Ellie's face fell. After all her hard work, after helping the Scrudges to win the auditions, they wouldn't let her come to London after all. She wouldn't get to swim in the Aquatics Centre.

"But you can't leave this little girl at home all on her own," said the television producer, looking horrified.

"The prize is for the whole family, or no one at all," the mayor added sternly.

"We were only joking," said Mrs Scrudge, forcing a laugh. "Weren't we, Ellie? Of course you can come, dearest."

Ellie knew they hadn't been joking, but she didn't care – they couldn't take it back now.

She gave Basil a high-five. Whisk jumped in the air and she stroked him.

She was going to London!

Chapter 4

It was the very next weekend, and Ellie knocked on the door of the big fancy suite in the big fancy hotel in London. Whisk yawned loudly – he had slept very well in the comfy hotel cat bed. Ellie's bed was comfy as well, but she was too excited to sleep. She planned to

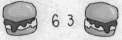

go to the Olympic Park with the Scrudges, then sneak off to the Aquatics Centre. It was open all day and Ellie wanted to spend as much time there as possible.

Mr Scrudge opened the door. "Oh, it's you," he said.

"Oh no, I hoped it was more room service," said Mrs Scrudge.

Their room was already littered with trays and trays of half-eaten food and expensive-looking drinks. It was only two hours until the competition and the Scrudges should have been on their way. But instead they were lounging in bed eating chocolate-covered strawberries.

"Your room is amazing!" Ellie gasped. It was the size of a flat, with its own little sitting room as well as a large balcony. She ran over to see the view.

"Of course our room is amazing," said Mrs Scrudge. "We won the competition. You're lucky we didn't ask the hotel manager to make you sleep in the supply cupboard."

Ellie shook her head in annoyance. "*I* won the competition with the cake that *I* made."

"And it was lucky your interfering didn't make us lose!" said Mr Scrudge.

Ellie ignored him – she wanted to see

the sights of London. The balcony had a perfect view of Buckingham Palace – the home of the Queen of England – and she was amazed at how big and beautiful it was. She liked the guards standing outside in their red uniforms and tall bearskin hats.

"I have always wanted to meet the Queen," Ellie said to herself.

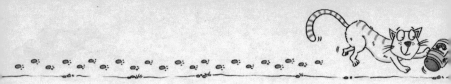

But Mr and Mrs Scrudge must have heard her because they started laughing.

"Did you hear that, Colin?" said Mr Scrudge, spit spraying out of his mouth as he laughed.

"The Queen wouldn't want to meet anyone as small and stupid as Ellie, would

she, Colin?" added Mrs Scrudge, who had
strawberry seeds stuck in her teeth.

Ellie turned to Colin, chin
up, ready to hear what he
had to say . . . but Colin
said nothing.

What's wrong with him?
she wondered. Colin had
been unusually quiet since
the auditions.

"I can't wait to see London," Ellie said.
"I've never been before. And the Olympic
Park is top of my list!"

Her aunt shrugged. "Do whatever you
like," she said, stuffing another chocolate

strawberry into her mouth. "But we don't want you at the competition."

"Yeah," said Mr Scrudge. "You'd only embarrass us."

They will be the ones embarrassing themselves if they don't at least try to make a decent cake! Ellie thought.

But she didn't need them to take her to the Olympic Park: Victoria Sponge had said she'd look after her. Ellie ran out of the Scrudges' suite and back to her own room, Whisk scampering behind her.

She went straight to the telephone to call her best friend. She knew that Basil would be excited when he heard what

she was doing today.

She rang his number and the phone rang
. . . and rang and rang. No one answered.
Still, she told herself, *I can tell him all about
it later.*

Instead, she opened her magical recipe
book.

"Victoria Sponge . . ." Ellie whispered, even though there was no one around except Whisk.

Victoria Sponge peeled herself out of the book. "What a lovely room, Ellie," she said.

"Isn't it gorgeous!" Ellie agreed. "There are views all over London.'

Ellie couldn't see Buckingham Palace from her room, but she loved looking at all the massive ancient buildings that surrounded the hotel. "London is so big it makes me feel even smaller than usual!" She chuckled at her own joke.

"How do you think *I* feel?" said Victoria

Sponge, laughing too. "I'm much smaller than you! But I've always loved London."

"Have you been here before?" asked Ellie.

"I used to work in a kitchen here," the magical baker told her.

Ellie was surprised. There was so much about Victoria Sponge that she didn't know.

"Your dad worked in London for a while too," Victoria continued.

Ellie gasped. She was about to ask more questions when there was a knock at the door.

"Who could that be?" she wondered.

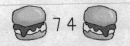

"I didn't order room service!"

Victoria Sponge hid behind the door as Ellie opened it. When Ellie saw who was there, her mouth fell open in amazement.

It was Basil – wearing a T-shirt with a monkey on it!

Whisk ran over and purred at him. He was as happy to see Basil as Ellie was.

"Basil!" said Victoria Sponge. "What a special surprise!"

Ellie hugged him so tightly that his glasses fell off. "What are you doing here?" she asked.

Basil picked up his glasses and put them back on. "My parents wanted to see Mr Patel compete in *Britain's Bestest Bakers*," he said. "So we've all come down to the Olympic Park."

"That's great!" said Ellie. "I'm going there too, but not for the competition. I'm going swimming in the Aquatics Centre." She was so excited she couldn't hide her smile.

"That's good – otherwise there would be no point in me bringing these." Basil held up his red swimming shorts with the dolphins on. "I'm coming with you!"

Ellie clapped her hands in delight.

"Let me just get my backpack."

Just then, there was another knock at the door.

"Are you sure you didn't order room service?" asked Victoria Sponge, hiding behind the door again.

Ellie opened the door, and her reaction was the complete opposite to that when Basil arrived: her mouth shut in disappointment.

It was Colin.

Whisk hissed at him from his cat bed.

"Sorry, Colin," said Ellie. "I'm afraid I don't have time to talk to you right now. So if you've just come to call me small and stupid—" But something about the look on Colin's face made her stop.

"Please, Ellie," he begged. "I need your help."

Chapter 5

Ellie frowned at Colin, not sure what to think. "You want me to help you?"

He nodded. "Please, Ellie. My parents are going to really embarrass me today," he begged. "They're no good at baking! They're too lazy to do it properly and . . . and . . ." He lowered his voice and he couldn't quite look Ellie in the eye as he said, "And even if they tried their hardest,

they'd never be as good as you."

Whisk almost fell out of his hotel cat bed in surprise.

Ellie folded her arms across her chest. "You've never admitted that before." She raised her eyebrow suspiciously. "Why now?"

"*Britain's Bestest Bakers* is on television! The Scrudges are going to be humiliated in front of the whole world."

"Maybe it will serve you right for being so horrible," Basil muttered. And for once, Colin didn't come back with a nasty reply.

"Please, Ellie," he begged again, clasping his hands together. "I know you

helped my parents win the auditions in Greyton."

Ellie couldn't help but smile when she thought of how much the judges had loved her cake. But should she help her cousin? She wasn't sure he deserved it. "You've always been mean to me,' she pointed out.

Colin gulped and looked down at his feet.

"Besides" – Basil stepped in front of Ellie, hands on his hips like the monkey on his T-shirt – "we're going swimming. We haven't got time to help you even if we wanted to."

Colin gulped and looked down at his feet. "I'm sorry I was mean to you, Ellie. You might be small, but you aren't stupid. I'm the stupid one for not realizing what a great cousin I have."

This time, Whisk *did* fall out of his bed in surprise.

"Have a fun day

swimming," he finished.

To her astonishment, Ellie saw a tear in his eye as he turned and headed off along the hotel corridor.

Basil slammed the door. "Ha! Serves him right," he said. "Finally the Scrudges get their just deserts."

Ellie always thought she'd feel happy when the Scrudges got what was coming to them . . . but she didn't.

"*Just deserts* – 'desserts' . . . get it?" said Basil, laughing at his own joke. "Because they're making cakes . . ."

Ellie sat down heavily on her bed.

Victoria Sponge fluttered over and hovered in front of her. "What's the matter, Ellie?" she asked.

"I know Colin and the Scrudges have never been nice to me, but Colin does seem very upset. What do you think I should do?" she asked. "Do you think I should help him?"

Victoria Sponge scratched her head with her wooden spoon. "You have to decide for yourself, Ellie," she said. "Do what you think is right."

It was something Ellie's dad used to say to her — that she should always follow her heart and do what she thought was the

right thing. But this time she wasn't sure what that was.

Basil came over and handed Ellie her backpack. "Come on," he said gently. "Swimming in the Aquatics Centre has always been your dream. Don't let the mean old Scrudges stand in your way."

Ellie came to a decision. She stood up and took the bag from Basil. "Yes," she

said. "Why should I change my plans for them?"

"Quite right!" Basil gave a firm nod that made his glasses slip down his nose.

Victoria Sponge hopped back into the magical recipe book.

Ellie popped the book into her bag and then strode out of her room and down to the hotel lobby, with Basil and Whisk marching along behind her.

There she found the Scrudges: Mrs Scrudge was carrying a plastic bucket in the shape of a castle, while Mr Scrudge had a bag full of grubby sand. What were they planning?

Colin trailed along behind them. He turned and saw Ellie and raised his hand to wave at her.

Ellie held her head high, but for some reason her heart felt very heavy.

"Hello there, Ellie!"

She turned to see Mr Patel rushing across the lobby.

"Hello, Mr Patel!" she said. "What are you doing here? Why aren't you preparing for *Britain's Bestest Bakers*?" She knew he wouldn't leave his preparations until the last minute – not like the Scrudges.

Mr Patel was gasping for breath. "I've been . . . there all . . . morning . . ." he

said, panting, "but I . . . had to . . . come back . . . to get changed."

"Why?" said Ellie. Mr Patel looked fine to her. There were a couple of chocolaty smudges on his apron, but that was to be expected when baking chocolate cake.

"Because they have revealed who

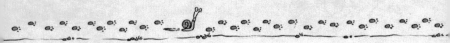

the secret VIP judge is going to be!" he said with an excited grin.

Ellie held her breath, waiting to hear the news.

"Is it an actor?" asked Basil.

"No," said Mr Patel.

"Is it a famous athlete?" asked Ellie.

"No – it's the Queen!"

Ellie gasped. Basil gasped. Whisk sneezed.

The Queen was going to be at the *Britain's Bestest Bakers* final! Ellie had always wanted to meet the Queen.

"Wowweee," said Basil.

And then Ellie remembered something else. Victoria Sponge had suggested making *Royal Tea for Royalty* for the auditions. This had to be a sign that Ellie should enter for the Scrudges.

Now she knew exactly the right thing to do.

She ran out of the hotel. The Scrudges were getting into a black London cab. "Colin! Wait!" she called.

Mrs Scrudge turned and scowled at her. "What do you want, Shrimp?"

"There's no room in our taxi," added Mr Scrudge. "Not even for a tiny shrimp like you."

Ellie ignored them and grabbed Colin by the arm. He bent down so she could whisper in his ear.

"I'll help you," she said.

Colin's smile filled his whole face. Even though they'd never got along, Ellie was

pleased to see her cousin so happy. Now she knew for certain that this was the right thing to do.

He hopped out of the taxi and headed back towards the hotel with her.

"Where do you think you're going?" said Mrs Scrudge.

"I'll meet you there," Colin called back to his parents. "I've just got to make something with Ellie first."

Mr and Mrs Scrudge frowned in confusion. "Why would you want to spend time with *her*?"

Colin and Ellie ignored them and hurried into the hotel lobby.

"Thank you, Ellie," said Colin. "You really are a brilliant cousin.'

Ellie smiled, and her heart felt lighter than it had for ages. Even if she never got to meet the Queen, or swim in the Aquatics Centre, becoming friends with her cousin would be the best surprise she'd had in ages.

Chapter 6

Heading through the lobby, Ellie found the door marked KITCHEN and knocked.

A man in a white apron and a tall white chef's hat opened it. He looked surprised when he saw Ellie, Basil, Colin and Whisk standing there.

"Can I help you?" he asked.

"We were wondering," Ellie said politely, "if we could use the hotel kitchen to

do some baking, please."

Basil stepped forward. "We're making tasty treats for the Queen!"

The chef smiled down at them. "If it's for the Queen, how can I refuse?"

Ellie was pretty sure the chef didn't believe Basil, but it didn't matter – he stood aside and let all four of them in anyway.

"Please feel free to help yourself to the ingredients in the pantry," he said. "There's a quiet little spot in the corner of the kitchen where you'll find all the equipment you need."

A quiet little spot was perfect – it meant that Ellie could let Victoria Sponge out of the book to help them bake. But there was one person she'd have to let in on the secret.

Ellie took the magical recipe book out of her bag and laid it on the worktop. "Colin," she said, suddenly full of self-confidence. Ellie knew what she was doing in a kitchen – no one could tell her she was

stupid when it came to baking.

Colin stood up straight.

"If I'm going to help you, you need to do exactly what I say and follow my instructions," Ellie told him.

Colin nodded.

"And no mean tricks or nasty name-calling," added Basil.

Colin shook his head. "I promise."

"And most importantly," said Ellie, lowering her voice to a whisper, "you must never ever tell anyone what I'm about to show you."

Colin shook his head again. "I double promise with cream on top," he said,

which made Ellie smile.

She pulled a stool over to the worktop and stood on it so that she could see properly. She opened the magical recipe book, and Victoria Sponge popped out with a puff of glittery sugar dust.

Colin's mouth fell wide open. "What...? How...? Who...?" he said, his mouth flapping like it was caught in a breeze.

"Hello," said Victoria Sponge, flying around Colin's head, making him turn in circles. "I'm Victoria Sponge. And you must be Colin."

Colin nodded, too stunned to speak. Ellie hid a giggle behind her hand – Colin's reaction was priceless!

"Are we going to make *Royal Tea for Royalty* again?" Victoria Sponge asked. "Scrumptious scones filled with cream and jam?"

Ellie nodded. "That's right. We're all here to help."

The four of them stood together, waiting for orders.

"Colin, you start whipping some

cream," Victoria Sponge said.

"Yes, Chef!" Colin said, sounding like he worked in a proper kitchen. He got a bowl out of the cupboard and some cream out of the fridge.

"Basil, you grease some baking trays."

Basil found some baking trays in a cupboard.

"And, Ellie, you find a big bowl and a spoon while I turn the oven on."

Ellie hopped off her stool and went to look for a wooden spoon and a bowl.

Whisk miaowed.

"Ah, Whisk," said Victoria Sponge. "You go and sniff out the finest strawberry

jam that London has to offer."

Whisk trotted off.

They all set to work. Colin was still whipping the cream when he turned to Ellie and asked, "Who is she?"

"Victoria Sponge is an old friend of my dad's," she explained. "They used to work together."

Ellie thought of her dad again now: she remembered his ginger beard, his round cheeks and his silly deep chuckle. Instantly she was surrounded by the aroma of freshly baked cakes. It always made her happy to think of him.

Next Ellie looked at the magical recipe book for the scone ingredients. "We need flour, butter and a pinch of salt," she said.

The flour was up on a high shelf. Ellie pursed her lips: it was too high for her to reach.

"I'll get that for you," offered Colin, without her asking.

Ellie saw the look on Basil's face change: he was clearly surprised by this new helpful Colin. This was the first time Colin had ever been nice to Ellie. Maybe it was the start of a friendship.

Ellie put the rest of the ingredients in the bowl.

"Don't forget my magical baking dust," said Victoria Sponge, and she tipped in a heaped spoonful.

The mixture began to glitter and twinkle.

"Wowweee," said Colin – then looked at Basil. "You don't mind me using your favourite word, do you, Basil?"

Basil smiled at him. "Not at all."

It wasn't long before the scones were ready. Whisk came back into the kitchen, rolling a jar of something in front of him.

When Ellie picked it up, she saw that it was a jar of tasty-looking strawberry jam.

"Where did you get this?" she asked him.

"Miaow," said Whisk, which wasn't much of an answer.

They prepared each scone with a thick layer of jam and a large dollop of the cream Colin had whipped. They looked delicious.

Ellie checked her watch. "We only have an hour to get to the Olympic Park!" she said. She had no idea if they would make it in time.

"Don't worry, I have some pocket money," said Colin. "I'll pay for us to get a taxi." He picked up the box of scones and carried them out of the hotel kitchen.

Ellie and Basil were thrilled to have a ride in a black cab. Ellie loved everything about it – from sitting backwards on the little flip-down seat to the orange light above the windscreen.

And then they were on their way to *Britain's Bestest Bakers*. Ellie was very excited. She loved competitions, but she was even more excited about actually seeing the Queen!

"Let's hold hands for luck," said Basil.

They all held hands, and Ellie took
Whisk's paw too.

The black cab whizzed through London,
and Ellie saw all the sights that she had
only ever seen on TV: Tower Bridge,
the London Eye, St Paul's Cathedral . . .
Finally they reached the Olympic Park.

"Look, Ellie!" said Basil, pointing at the wavy roof of the Aquatics Centre. "There it is!" Then he leaned in close and whispered into her ear, "Are you sorry you won't be able to swim in it?"

Ellie did feel a pang of sadness, but only a small one. As she looked down at her hand resting in Colin's, she thought it might just be worth missing out on her special swim – she had made a new friend today.

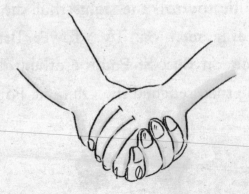

Chapter 7

Walking into the Olympic Stadium made Ellie feel dizzy. It was bigger than anything she had ever seen before – much bigger than Greyton Green. And there were rows and rows of seating which held tens of thousands of spectators. There was no ceiling above them, and the bright sunshine streamed in through the open roof.

But this wasn't the only thing that made Ellie's head spin. It was all the sights and smells of the amazing tasty treats that surrounded her. Cupcakes, fluffy pastries, mountains of doughnuts, tons of tarts — too many for Ellie to take in. And they all looked delicious. Someone nearby had made a banana cake — Ellie could smell it.

She spotted Mr Patel at his table. He had made another Chocolate Perfection

Pie, but this one looked ten times bigger and twenty times tastier than the last.

Basil scratched his head, looking worried. "There's no way we can win against all these people," he said.

Colin – still carrying the boxes of scones – smiled at Ellie. "It was never about winning," he told her. "I just didn't want to have to stand by one of my parents' disgusting-looking cakes. Not when

everyone else has tried so hard."

"You're right, Colin," said Ellie. "We tried our best and we should be proud of what we've done."

An announcement came over the loudspeaker: "Contestants, you have five minutes before judging begins! Look out for the television cameras."

An anxious gasp went up as everyone hurried to add the finishing touches to their bakes. The woman with the banana cake was slicing some fresh bananas so frantically that she didn't notice the skins falling on the floor.

Mr and Mrs Scrudge were easy to find.

As usual, theirs was the table everyone seemed to be avoiding. Mrs Scrudge had applied lots of bright pink make-up and was batting her eyelashes at a camera.

"Coo-eee!" she called out to the television producers. "I don't believe you've filmed us yet. I'm also available for modelling work, if you're interested."

The camera turned away sharply.

Mr Scrudge stood behind his creation. He had poured sand into the bucket and tipped it out to make a Sandcastle Cake. But the sand had dried out and was crumbling.

"Dad said it would be easier to make a sandcastle than a cake . . . but they didn't even bother to take out the shells," Colin admitted.

Just then, a crab crawled out of the middle of the cake.

"Yuck!" said Ellie.

Another contestant caught sight of it and pulled a disgusted face.

Mr Scrudge growled. "What are you

staring at?" he said. The woman turned away and hurried off.

"Mum! Dad!" Colin called over. "Quick – we don't have long."

Ellie could see the television producer with the pencil behind her ear making

notes as the presenter started speaking to camera.

"Colin! There you are," said Mr Scrudge. "I need you to go up to the judges and tell them that if we don't win, there'll be serious trouble."

Ellie was about to tell him that one of the judges was the Queen: if he tried to threaten *her*, he'd end up in jail! But Mr Scrudge caught sight of Ellie and scowled. "What did you bring *her* for? She's only going to embarrass us."

Ellie scowled right back. It was *they* who were embarrassing Colin.

Colin set their box down on the table.

"Quick," he said. "We need to swap your . . . erm . . . cake for these scrumptious scones."

Mr Scrudge frowned. "We're not swapping. You've never baked in your life – why would we use your scones?"

Colin shook his head. "I didn't make them myself," he said. "I had help from

someone wonderful. Someone very, very little. Someone who does magic."

Ellie exchanged a worried look with Basil. "Oh no," she whispered to him. "He's going to tell them about Victoria Sponge. The secret will be out!"

Basil shook his head. "I knew Colin couldn't be trusted!"

"Who is this magical little person?" asked Mr Scrudge, folding his arms across his chest and gazing at Colin in disbelief.

"Ellie," said Colin.

Ellie did a double-take. So did Mr and Mrs Scrudge.

"What?" said Mrs Scrudge. "The shrimp?"

"Yes," said Colin, opening the box and showing his parents. "Ellie made these scones. Her cakes are always really yummy and I think we should

use them instead. Your cake will taste disgusting and we'll look stupid on TV."

Ellie felt herself blushing with pride. Not only had Colin kept her secret – he had given her all the credit for the delicious scones.

"Colin helped too," she said. "And Basil. And even Whisk lent a paw."

Mr Scrudge scoffed, but Mrs Scrudge wiped her lips because her mouth was watering.

"I don't know," said Mr Scrudge, eyeing the scones. "Wouldn't it be easier to force the judges to let us win?"

"I really think—" Ellie started. But she was interrupted by a loud fanfare

trumpeting through the hall.

Ellie turned to see a group of people – including men and women in suits, photographers, and guards in red uniforms and tall bearskin hats – surrounding a woman with grey hair. She wasn't wearing her crown; instead she had a yellow dress

123

and jacket, and a matching yellow hat and handbag.

The Queen!

Mr Patel was right – the Queen was the secret VIP judge. Ellie couldn't believe she was seeing her in real life. It was a dream come true.

She watched as the television producer cut slices of cake and gave them to the Queen. The Queen took a small bite of each one and smiled politely. Ellie wondered what she really thought of everyone's entries.

The voice on the loudspeaker started up again: "As you can see, Her Majesty the Queen has started judging today's entries.

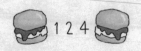

The winner will receive a thousand pounds!"

Mr Scrudge's eyes snapped open as if he'd just remembered the prize. "We *have* to win!" He started drooling over the money, just like Mrs Scrudge had drooled over Ellie's scones. He quickly tipped the Sandcastle Cake onto the floor. Then he grabbed the plate of scones and pushed it in front of him.

"Quickly!" Mrs Scrudge screeched. "She's here!"

The Queen stood just centimetres away from Ellie. Ellie was a little light-headed – she didn't know what to say. But when the Queen smiled down at her,

Ellie felt herself relaxing.

"Are these your scones?" the Queen asked. "They look delicious."

"Well . . ." Ellie started. She wished she could tell her the truth, that they were her scones. But she had made a promise to Colin.

"No!" said Mr Scrudge. "They're ours. We made them. Ourselves."

"Don't worry, Your Majesty," added Mrs

Scrudge in a sickly sweet voice. "We don't let that little shrimp get her dirty hands on our food."

"Actually, Ellie made—" Colin said, but his parents cut him off with a glare.

The Queen picked up a scone and looked at it. She smiled, then took a bite. A splodge of cream squeezed out of the side, but she delicately wiped it away with a napkin.

She opened her mouth again, about to take another bite, but then stopped herself. "I'd better not," she said, looking around at all the tables. "I have so many other cakes to try." She turned and looked at

Ellie. "This is delicious – well done."

It was as if she knew that the Scrudges hadn't made the scones. Ellie felt very proud.

As soon as the Queen had left, Mr Scrudge threw his tea towel down on the table in disgust. "Did you see that? She could only stomach one bite. We're never going to win with these stupid scones!" he said.

"I don't know, Dad . . ." Colin said.

"Ellie's scones were much nicer than

your cake would have been," added Basil.

"There's no point in hanging around here if we're not going to win first prize," Mr Scrudge said, heading away from the table.

"It's not the winning," said Ellie, "it's the taking part that counts."

"Pah!" said Mr Scrudge. "What a stupid thing to say!"

"I'm going back to the hotel to eat more chocolate," said Mrs Scrudge.

"Come on, Colin, let's go. Ellie can clean up this mess."

"I'll stay and help her," Colin said.

"Colin, now!" growled Mr Scrudge.

"It's OK, Colin," said Ellie. "You go. I don't mind."

Mr and Mrs Scrudge stomped off past the table with the amazing smelling banana cake. Mr Scrudge slipped on one of the banana skins, falling flat on his big bum.

The cameras turned to film it.

"Ow!" he cried, his face bright red. "Help me up."

"No," hissed Mrs Scrudge. "I'm trying to pretend I don't know you. How else will I get my modelling career going?" She carried on walking, wiggling her fat bottom . . . then slipped on another banana skin and landed next to Mr Scrudge.

"That's going on the out-take reel!" the television producer said to the cameraman.

Colin looked at his parents; he was laughing but trying to hide it.

"Sorry about them," he said to Ellie. "And thanks so much for helping me. I would have hated to embarrass myself in

front of the Queen." Then he helped his
mum and dad up.

Basil found a dustpan and brush and
began sweeping up the sand from the
Sandcastle Cake. Whisk was licking up

the cream that had escaped from the scones. Ellie got a cloth and started wiping the table.

"I don't know if it was worth missing the Aquatics Centre for this," said Basil with a sigh. "We got to see the Queen, but the Scrudges didn't appreciate your help, did they, Ellie? They didn't even say thank you!"

Ellie continued wiping, with a smile on her face. "But Colin appreciated it," she said.

The Aquatics Centre would be around for the rest of her life. She could come back another time. But she'd made friends with

her cousin Colin and he was becoming a nicer person. That made the whole day worthwhile.

Chapter 8

By the time Ellie, Basil and Whisk had finished cleaning up the Scrudges' mess, the stadium was almost empty. Through the open roof, Ellie could see the setting sun. It looked beautiful, but that wasn't what was making her smile. Mr Patel had won first prize, and while Basil stayed to help Ellie, Basil's parents were taking Mr Patel out to tea to celebrate. She was

thrilled for him. His Chocolate Perfection Pie definitely deserved to win.

She swept the last of the sand into the dustpan and felt someone tap her on the shoulder.

Ellie turned and came face to face with a yellow handbag. When she looked up, she saw the Queen standing next to her.

She was amazed, but remembered to curtsey. "Hello, Your Majesty . . . Your Highness . . . Your Queenliness . . . Your . . . erm . . ."

The Queen smiled. "Call me *Ma'am*. To rhyme with *jam*."

Basil had frozen on the spot. So had

Whisk. They just stared. Ellie hoped the Queen didn't think they were being rude.

"It's actually jam that I came to speak to you about," the Queen said.

Ellie gulped. "Really?"

The Queen nodded. "The Chocolate

Perfection Pie has always been a favourite of mine, and my children's, and my grandchildren's, and even my great-grandchildren's! It was so tasty I just had to choose it as the winner. I hope you weren't too disappointed."

"Not at all!" said Ellie. "It's the taking part, not the winning that counts."

"Quite!" The Queen nodded again. "But I did want to tell you that I thought your entry – the jam, the cream, the scrumptious scones –

was absolutely delicious! Well done!"

Ellie beamed, then tried to hide it. After all, she had to pretend that the Scrudges had made the scones. "Thank you very much, Ma'am. I'll let my aunt and uncle know."

The Queen raised a gloved finger and winked at Ellie. "I know it was you who made them."

"But . . ." Ellie couldn't bring herself to deny it. "How?"

"A young boy ran over to tell me, just before his parents dragged him outside," she said. "His name was Colin. And he said you were the bestest baker he had ever met."

Ellie couldn't believe Colin had said that about her. It was so nice of him.

"I don't suppose . . ." said the Queen. "Do you have any left? I would love another one."

"But of course, Ma'am!" said Ellie. She reached into the box and handed the Queen a scone.

The Queen took a big un-delicate bite. This time, when the cream splodged out of

the side, she licked it off with her tongue. "Delicious!" she exclaimed. "It reminds me of the tasty treats one of the bakers in the palace used to make for me. Though that was a long time ago." She looked up at the sky thoughtfully. "I can't quite remember his name, but he had rosy cheeks and

a silly deep chuckle. He was a wonderful baker."

Ellie gasped. *Could the Queen be talking about my dad?!* she wondered.

Instantly she was surrounded by the aroma of freshly baked cakes.

It was the Queen's turn to gasp. "Do you smell that? The aroma of freshly baked cakes?"

She smelled it too!

Then the Queen bent down and whispered in Ellie's ear, "The baker had a magical little friend. I would love to see her again one day."

Ellie was now certain who she was talking about. "Just a moment," she said with a smile. She got out the magical recipe book and opened it on the table. "Victoria Sponge," she whispered.

Victoria Sponge appeared, and when she saw the Queen she gave a deep curtsey. "Hello, Ma'am," she said. "How lovely to see you again."

"How lovely to see you too, Victoria Sponge!" the Queen exclaimed. "How are you? Still cooking up brilliant bakes?"

"I am," said Victoria Sponge. "With lots of help from Ellie, Basil, and Ellie's little cat, Whisk."

The Queen reached down and stroked Whisk's ears. Basil was still standing frozen in shock.

"Ellie is going to be a great baker. Just as good as her dad," Victoria Sponge continued. "I wonder if she'll work in the palace kitchens one day . . . just like him."

Ellie could hardly believe it. Her dad had worked in Buckingham Palace!

"Ellie's an amazing swimmer too!" Basil blurted out. He'd finally found his tongue.

They all turned to hear what he had to say.

"We wanted to go to the Aquatics Centre today . . . but" – he checked his watch – "I think it must be closed by now."

The Queen smiled an intriguing smile.

"I wonder if I can help there," she said. "It is called the *Queen Elizabeth* Olympic Park, after all!"

Ellie powered through the water, kicking her legs and making windmills with her arms. She kept her head

down, only turning it when she needed
to breathe.

"Come on, Ellie!" she heard when her
head popped above the waves.

"Go! Go! Go!" It was Colin, cheering
her on.

Ellie reached the end of the pool and
sprang up to see the time on the
stopwatch.

The Aquatics Centre was
the most amazing place she
had ever seen. The roof was
higher than the hotel and the
pool was the largest she had ever
swum in. There were high diving boards

at one end, but Ellie just wanted to swim. The Queen had granted them special access to the pool, and her chauffeur had driven them all there, stopping to pick up Colin on the way. Ellie, Basil, Colin, Whisk and Victoria Sponge were the only people in the Aquatics Centre.

"How was my time?" Ellie asked.

Basil looked at his stopwatch. "Your personal best!" he told her.

"You really are an amazing swimmer," said Colin. "You should enter the Olympics!"

Ellie smiled to herself. She might just do that.

Her trip to London had been the best ever. She had fulfilled her dream of meeting the Queen and swimming in the Aquatics Centre at the Olympic Park.

And best of all, she was now friends with her cousin Colin. All thanks to her scrumptious scones.

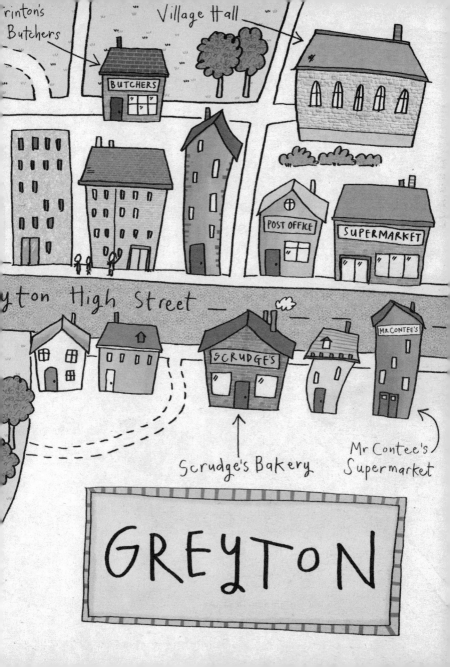

Read on for
a sneak peek of
Ellie's first
baking adventure!

Ellie's Magical Bakery

Best Cake for a Best Friend

♥ ELLIE SIMMONDS ♥

Illustrated by Kimberley Scott

RED FOX

Chapter 1

It was the morning of Ellie's birthday. Before she stepped into Scrudge's Bakery she took a deep breath to give herself courage . . . then wished she hadn't. The bakery smelled like old socks and soggy cabbage. *Revolting, as usual*, Ellie thought.

She looked around the bakery, hoping she might have a birthday present. The shelves were lined with week-old bread,

stale, stodgy cakes and mouldy muffins. Her uncle, Mr Scrudge, stood behind one of the shop counters mixing cookie dough. Ellie watched as he shoved a fistful of chocolate chips into his mouth, then swept a handful of dead flies off the worktop and into the dough. *Yuck!*

And there was no sign of a present.

Ellie knew very little about her mum,
and her dad had died three years ago.
She remembered his ginger beard, round
cheeks and silly deep chuckle. Whenever
she thought about him she was surrounded
by the aroma of freshly baked cakes
. . . not this horrible smell! Her aunt
and uncle ran her father's bakery now.

They had changed the name of the shop to 'Scrudge's Bakery' and had moved into the flat above it with Ellie and her ginger cat, Whisk.

She hadn't had a birthday present since.

Mrs Scrudge was slouching in a chair behind the till, her belly squeezing out of the top of her trousers. "What do *you* want, Shrimp?" she asked Ellie, straining to reach a mug of tea.

Ellie passed her the mug. There *was* something she wanted — even more than a present. She was going

to ask her aunt and uncle
for a special birthday treat.

Whisk ran over and
rubbed up against her leg.
It gave her courage.

"Umm, it's my birth—"
she started to say.

But the door to the shop suddenly
opened and a man walked in.

"Customers! Quiet!" hissed Mrs Scrudge,
and heaved herself up in her chair.

Whisk hissed. Ellie stroked his fur and
looked up to see who it was. Customers
were rare since the Scrudges had taken
over the bakery. It was Mr Amrit,

a man she'd seen around the village. Clearly he hadn't heard how awful the food was here.

He strode up to the counter confidently, then caught sight of the horrible-looking cakes, cringed, and held his nose.

"Hello, sir," Mrs Scrudge simpered, batting her eyelashes. "Do buy something from our delightful shop."

"Er . . . no thank you," said Mr Amrit, backing out of the door. "I've just remembered, I . . ."

Ellie went to hold the door for him – she couldn't blame Mr Amrit for wanting to leave. But her aunt lunged forward

and grabbed Ellie's arm while her uncle blocked poor Mr Amrit's exit. Mr Scrudge was huge – the size of a garden shed – with stubble on his face and neck.

"Buy something from our delightful shop," he growled. "Or else!" He put up his fist.

Mr Amrit cowered, then forced a smile onto his face. "My wife *is* partial to carrot cake," he said, his voice shaking with fear. "D-d-do you have some?"

Mrs Scrudge gave him a slice of cake. It was furrier than Whisk.

"Do you think that's safe to eat?" Ellie asked her aunt. "It looks a bit green."

"'Course it's green," Mrs Scrudge snapped.

"It's Brussels sprout cake."

Ellie winced.

Mr Amrit winced.

Even Whisk winced.

Who would want to eat a Brussels sprout cake?

"It was *carrot* cake I was after," Mr Amrit said. "You know, with the creamy white icing—'

Mr Scrudge raised his fists again and Mr Amrit said, "But this looks nice too." He took the cake, handed over his money and hurried out of the shop.

"Come back soon!" called Mrs Scrudge, then she slumped back in her chair, puffing from the effort.

Ellie felt terribly sorry for Mr Amrit. Cakes were supposed to be delicious, tasty treats. The Scrudges' definitely weren't.

She'd never dared eat any of their cakes – not since she'd heard worrying gurgly noises coming from the tummies of the villagers who had. But when Ellie was younger, her dad had let her help in the

bakery. She wanted to try baking again – to make her very own birthday cake.

"Uncle," she said. "It's my birth—"

"I'm busy!" he yelled at her. But he was only busy cleaning out his ears with his finger.

"I could help you in the bakery if you like." Ellie pulled her long brown hair into a ponytail, ready to get stuck in.

Mr Scrudge turned and laughed. "Don't be ridiculous!"

Mrs Scrudge laughed too. "You are too small and too stupid to make cakes. In fact, you're too small and too stupid to do anything."

Ellie crossed her arms in front of her chest. She *was* small. She had a condition called achondroplasia, which meant she was shorter than most people.

171

But there was no such thing as *too small*.
An ant can lift things fifty times heavier
than itself. A salmon swims thousands of
miles. Even the smallest birthday present
can make a person very happy.

And Ellie was most certainly *not* stupid.

"But if you would like to prove you're not completely useless," Mrs Scrudge said, "go to the garden centre and get me some cement mix. I can't be bothered."

"Why do you need cement mix?" Ellie asked.

"It's cheaper than flour," her aunt replied.

"And mud is cheaper than chocolate," added Mr Scrudge.

Yuck!

"Can't Colin go?" Ellie asked. Colin was her cousin, the Scrudges' twelve-year-old son.

"No," said Mrs Scrudge. "He's out."

Ellie was certain Colin *was* out: he was

173

probably out bullying someone.

"Fine," she said. It was annoying how lazy the Scrudges were, but she was pleased to have an excuse to get away from them.

"Make sure you're back by four," Mr Scrudge called after her. "Or I'll put Whiskers in the next batch!" He threw a burned bun at Ellie's cat.

Whisk miaowed, annoyed.

Ellie snapped back, "My cat's name is *Whisk*!"

"What's a whisk?" said Mrs Scrudge.

Ellie shook her head in dismay – any baker should know what a whisk was!

She held the door open for the cat as they left the shop.

Then she stumbled.

At first she assumed that Colin had left something on the ground on purpose, to trip her up; he'd done that before. But when she looked down, she gasped with surprise. There on the doorstep lay a neatly wrapped present about the size of a pizza box. It had a bow on it, the paper was covered in pictures of cupcakes with candles on, and the words *Happy Birthday Ellie* were written on the front.

"Do you think the Scrudges have bought me a birthday present after all?" Ellie wondered aloud. But deep down she knew that there was more chance of Whisk buying her a present than Mr and Mrs Scrudge.

There was a note on the front that said:

Open in secret

Ellie knew just the place . . .

Turn the page
for lots of fun
Ellie's Magical Bakery
activities!

A Queenly Quiz!

1. Which three animals appear on the front of Basil's t-shirts?

2. What type of hat do the Royal Guards wear?

3. What colour is the Queen's outfit?

4. What tasty treat are Mr and Mrs Scrudge eating in bed on the day of the competition?

5. Which key ingredient does Whisk collect for the Royal Tea?

6. What do Mr and Mrs Scrudge slip up on in the Britain's Bestest Baker final?

7. What does Mr Patel call his winning dessert?

8. Which title does Ellie use to address the Queen?

9. Where does Ellie eventually get to go for a swim in London?

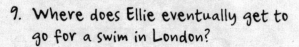

Answers: dog, cow, monkey; Bearskins; yellow; chocolate-covered strawberries; strawberry jam; banana skins; Chocolate Perfection Pie; Madam; the Aquatics Centre in the London Olympic Park

Hello, lovely to see you!

Do you like to bake?

Why don't you try out Ellie's recipe?

Make sure you always have a grown-up around to help.

When the scones are ready, why don't you invite some friends over to share them with you?

Happy Baking!

Victoria Sponge

Make your own
Royal Tea for Royalty
with this Scrumptious
Scone Recipe

Makes about 16 small scones

Ingredients:

200g clotted cream

100g strawberry jam

225g self-raising flour (plus a little
extra to cover your rolling surface)

25g caster sugar

1 egg

50g butter (plus a little extra
for greasing)

1 teaspoon of salt

115ml milk (plus a bit more to brush
on your scones before baking)

Top Tip If you like fruit scones,
simply add 2 large handfuls of raisins
to the flour before mixing!

Utensils:

baking tray

large bowl

rolling pin

wooden spoon

pastry brush

4cm round
pastry cutter

aprons

cooling rack

1. Put on your aprons and pre-heat the oven to 200°C.

2. Use the extra butter to lightly grease your baking tray.

3. In the large bowl, mix together the flour, sugar and salt then, using your fingers, rub in the butter until the mixture looks like breadcrumbs.

4. Slowly add the milk to the mixture, stirring it until it forms a soft smooth dough.

5. Tip the dough out onto a lightly floured surface and roll out to a thickness of 2-3cm, and use your cutter to cut out your scones.

Top Tip Keep re-rolling any leftover bits of dough until it's all used up!

6. Arrange each scone on your greased baking tray before lightly brushing the tops with the extra milk.

7. Ask your adult helper to place your scones in the oven for about 10-15 minutes or until they have risen well and are golden in colour.

8. When they're ready, ask your adult helper to get them out of the oven. Leave them for about 3 minutes before placing them on your cooling rack.

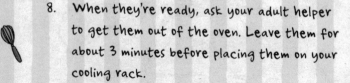

9. When cool to the touch, halve your scones and spread a teaspoonful of jam on the bottom half and a tablespoonful of clotted cream on the top half of each scone. Put the two halves together and serve with a lovely cup of tea!

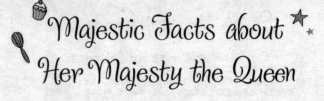

Majestic Facts about Her Majesty the Queen

* The Queen has four children, eight grand-children, five great-grandchildren and 30 god-children.

* The Queen's most famous crown is the Imperial State Crown, and its many gems include 2,868 diamonds, 273 pearls, 17 sapphires, 11 emeralds, and five rubies.

* The Queen celebrates two birthdays every year! She spends her actual birthday on 21 April with her family, then celebrates her official birthday on a Saturday in June, with a ceremony that includes the Horse Guards Parade and a garden party.

* The Queen has owned more than 30 dogs, all of them Corgis.

* The Queen's full official title is 'Her Majesty Elizabeth the Second, by the Grace of God of the United Kingdom of Great Britain and Northern Ireland, and of Her Other Realms and Territories Queen, Head of the Commonwealth, Defender of the Faith'.

Spot the Difference

Can you spot five differences
between these two pictures?

ELLIE SIMMONDS is a Paralympic swimming champion and has ten world records to her name. At 14, Ellie was the youngest recipient of the MBE, and also now has an OBE – both special titles awarded by the Queen. Ellie has continued to succeed in swimming, but she also loves to bake! Working on Ellie's Magical Bakery is a really exciting new way for Ellie to pursue her love of cakes and bakes.

Ellie's disability is called Achondroplasia (dwarfism). Achondroplasia means that Ellie has shorter arms and legs than most people. As a result Ellie is a lot smaller than other people her age, but this has never stopped her from doing the things she loves the most.

KIMBERLEY SCOTT is a professional illustrator and designer. She regularly works on a diverse range of projects and loves to delve into imaginative worlds. Kimberley lives and works in London, from her teeny-weeny studio, with a constant supply of green tea and pick-and-mix sweets to keep her creativity flowing!